The KNIGHTS Before CHRISTMAS

Joan Holub

Illustrated by
Scott Magoon

Christy Ottaviano Books

HENRY HOLT AND COMPANY

NEW YORK

For Kristen S. and Paul H.
—J. H.

For everyone who lets the spirit of
Christmas invade their hearts. Merry Christmas!
—S. M.

Henry Holt and Company, LLC
Publishers since 1866
175 Fifth Avenue, New York, New York 10010
mackids.com

Henry Holt® is a registered trademark of Henry Holt and Company, LLC.
Text copyright © 2015 by Joan Holub
Illustrations copyright © 2015 by Scott Magoon
All rights reserved.

Henry Holt books may be purchased for business or promotional use. For information
on bulk purchases, please contact the Macmillan Corporate and Premium Sales Department
at (800) 221-7945 x5442 or by e-mail at specialmarkets@macmillan.com.

Library of Congress Cataloging-in-Publication Data
Holub, Joan.
The knights before Christmas / Joan Holub ; illustrated by Scott Magoon.
pages   cm
"Christy Ottaviano Books."
Summary: "'Twas December 24th, and three brave knights were just settling in for the night when out
on the drawbridge, there arose such a clatter! The knights try everything to get rid of this unknown invader
(Santa Claus!), a red and white knight with a fleet of dragons"—Provided by publisher.
ISBN 978-0-8050-9932-4 (hardback)
[1. Stories in rhyme. 2. Santa Claus—Fiction. 3. Christmas—Fiction. 4. Knights and knighthood—Fiction.
5. Castles—Fiction.] I. Magoon, Scott, illustator. II. Title.
PZ8.3.H74Kn 2015   [E]—dc23   2014042198

First Edition—2015 / Designed by April Ward
The artwork was created digitally in Adobe Photoshop.
Printed in China by RR Donnelley Asia Printing Solutions Ltd., Dongguan City, Guangdong Province

1 3 5 7 9 10 8 6 4 2

Polite Knight, with his pen,
issued dire decrees.

"Keep out of our keep!"

"No ransackers, please!"

Don't Hassle our Castle!

Do not float in our moat!

Begone from our Lawn!

Invaders have fleas!

Marauders: Take Baths!

Silent Knight, in his nightie
and iron-armored cap,
was just settling in
for a long winter's nap.

*I'm dreaming
of a white javelin,
just like the one
I used to throw . . .*

Then out on the drawbridge
there arose such a clatter,
those knights sprang to the tower
to see what was the matter.

SIR
KNIGHTIE
KNIGHT

SIR
DANCE-
A-LOT

SIR
KNIGHT
STAND

Yeah! Keep your boots on, already!

When what to their wondering eyes
should appear,
but a red-and-white knight
and eight dragons. Oh dear!

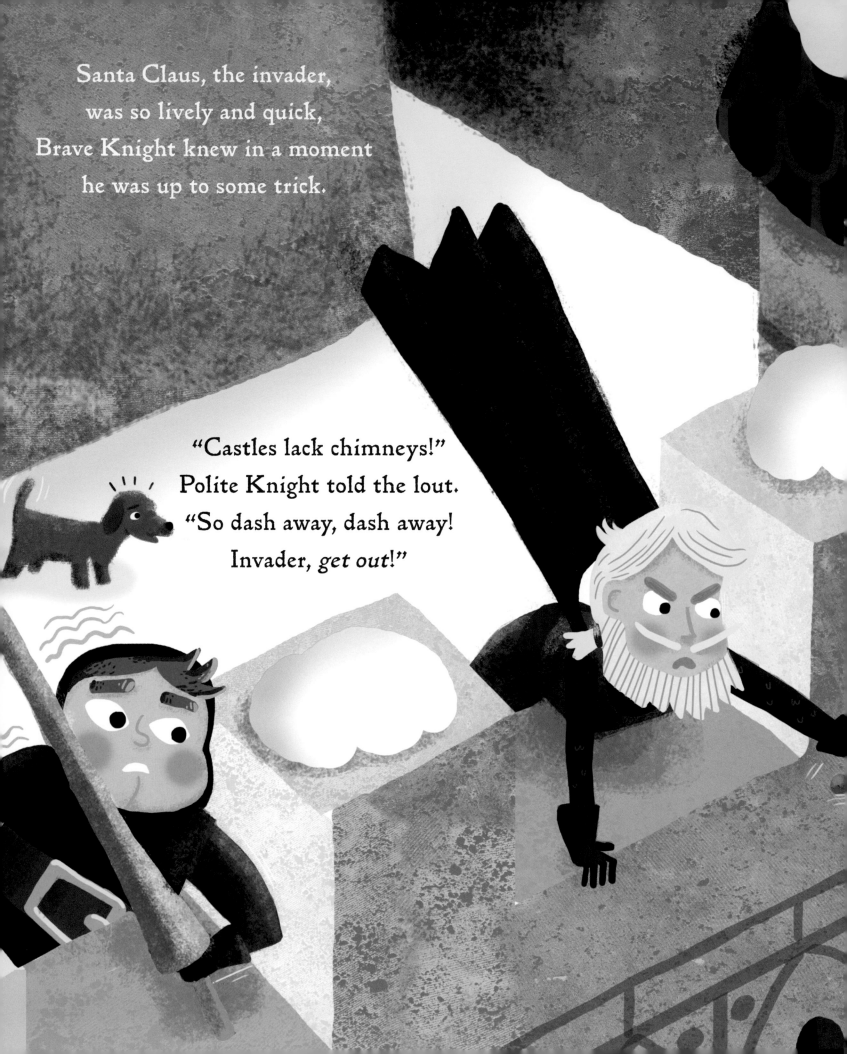

Santa Claus, the invader,
was so lively and quick,
Brave Knight knew in a moment
he was up to some trick.

"Castles lack chimneys!"
Polite Knight told the lout.
"So dash away, dash away!
Invader, *get out!*"

Alas, the invader
would not go.

Ho! Ho!
Ho!

From the top of the wall
the knight trio flew
to consult the king's book
on what good knights should do.

CHAPTER XI

So You Want to
REPEL
INVADERS

I.
Draw the bridge.

II.
Fill the moat, then throw them in irons.

III.
Strike the coat of arms.

Brave Knight
drew the bridge.

Fill moat?
Check.
Throw irons?
Check.

Polite Knight
filled the moat.

Silent Knight duked it out
with a many-armed coat.

But nothing would stop
their white-whiskered foe.
No matter their efforts,
he just would not go!

Open up, knights!
It's Christmas Eve.

For Santa Claus had a list.
And he'd checkmarked it thrice.
He knew that their deeds
had been chivalrous and nice.

Anne the Cone-Headed

Bob the Fowl

Tom of Camelot

Brave Knight

Polite Knight

Silent Knight of the Iron Underwear

End of List

Yes! He would conquer their castle
with the bounty in his sack.
"You can't stop me," he told them.
"So, good knights—STAND BACK!"

The knights dove from the battlements,
hiding under their beds,
as dozens of sugarplums
rained down on their heads.

Three shields came in camouflage.
Mint spears hit the gate,
as Santa stormed that castle
with his fierce dragons eight.

More rapid than eagles,
bows and arrows, they flew.
There were whistles and horns,
men of gingerbread, too.

That volley of goodies
those knights flung right back.
But then Santa hurled more
from inside his sack!

Just when all appeared lost,
a bleak silence fell.
The knights peeked out . . . and cheered.
They'd WON! All was well!

The invader was gone.
And in his haste to flee,
he'd forgotten his catapult.
Yay! VICTORY!

Those knights brought it in
and festooned it with holly.
Decked with treats of their triumph,
it looked oh so jolly.

They gathered 'round it singing,
for their joy was vast.
They'd driven away
the invader—at last!

Then they heard Santa call
as he flew out of sight:
"Merry Christmas to all
And to all, nighty knight!"